NAMING MONSTERS

Naming Monsters

HANNAH EATON

First published in 2013 by

Myriad Editions
59 Lansdowne Place
Brighton BN3 1FL, UK

www.myriadeditions.com

1 3 5 7 9 10 8 6 4 2

A CIP catalogue record for this book is available from the British Library.

ISBN: 978-1-908434-21-0

Printed in Lithuania on paper sourced from sustainable forests.

Contents

Prologue 9

The Changeling 19

The Kappa 29

The Black Dog 47

The Golem 61

The Incubus 77

The Bannik 89

The Boggart 107

The Brag 123

Nuckelavee 137

Laying Ghosts 151

Afterword 173

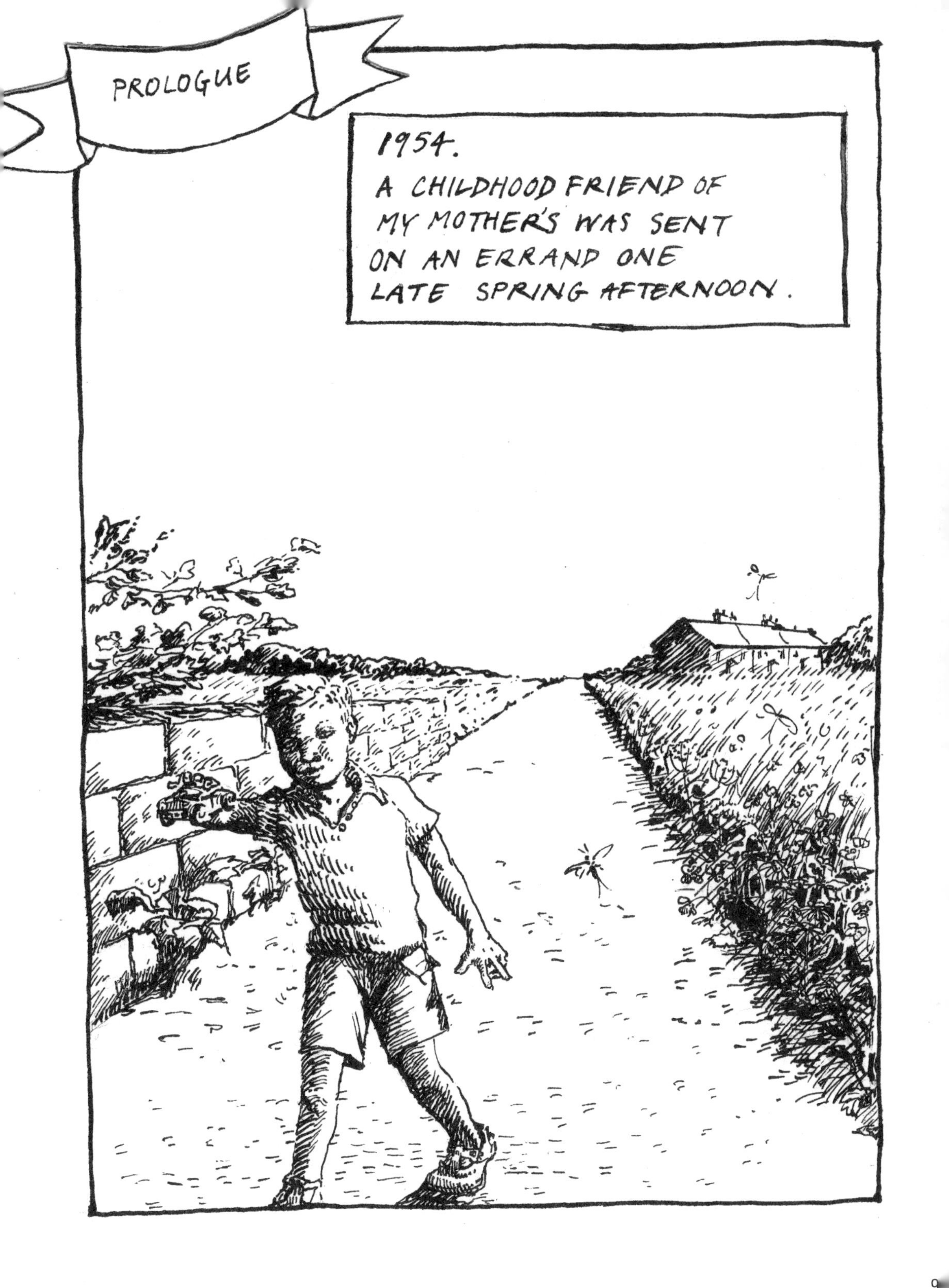
PROLOGUE
1954.
A CHILDHOOD FRIEND OF MY MOTHER'S WAS SENT ON AN ERRAND ONE LATE SPRING AFTERNOON.

HE LEFT THE SHOP AND HEADED DOWN THE VILLAGE STREET...
...TO THE LANE THAT LED TO THE CHURCH.
IN THE SHADE OF THE LYCH-GATE, ALL OF A SUDDEN...

A BIG BLACK DOG ROSE UP, OUT OF NOWHERE,
AND PUT ITS PAWS ON HIS SMALL SHOULDERS.

HIS ERRAND FORGOTTEN, HE WANDERED HOME TO HIS MOTHER...
WHO SAID THERE HAD BEEN SOMETHING ODD ABOUT HIM, LIKE A SMELL PERHAPS, OR A TAINT.
SHE GAVE HIM SOME ICE-CREAM AND SENT HIM TO BED.
FIVE HAVE PLENTY OF FUN
KILLER CHRISTIE

IN THE MORNING, HE WAS DEAD.

I ASSURE YOU I AM NOT SHOWING OFF WHEN I SAY I AM PROBABLY THE COUNTRY'S PRE-EMINENT TEENAGE CRYPTOZOOLOGIST.
ACTUALLY, THAT ISN'T THE RIGHT WORD. I THINK A CRYPTOZOOLOGIST MIGHT BE ONE OF THOSE PEOPLE WHO STAND AROUND IN KHAKI WAISTCOATS GETTING AROUSED ABOUT YETIS.
ADESH
FRUITERER
SIMONS
0171 39235
Chicken

I MUST BE A MONSTEROLOGIST, THEN.
THAT'S NO LESS EMBARRASSING,
BUT IT CAN'T BE HELPED.
87
I HAVE KNOWN NOW FOR A
YEAR OR SO – A YEAR LAST APRIL,
TO BE EXACT:
MONSTERS ARE ALL AROUND US.

KURT COBAIN
AND TO BE INFORMED IS TO BE PREPARED, I SAY.
BAD THINGS HAPPEN TO THE UNPREPARED.
THAT STORY... THAT LITTLE BOY...
KURT CO
GHOSTS
WORLD MYTHOLOGY
IT MAY SEEM LIKE A STRANGE STORY; SMALL AND SAD...
... BUT IT'S ALL TRUE.
ENGLISH FOLKLORE

OBVIOUSLY, THE PARENTS NEVER GOT OVER IT.
YOU SEE?
MONSTERS ARE ALL AROUND US.

THE CHANGELING
IT HAS BEEN KNOWN FOR THE FAIRIES TO STEAL A HUMAN CHILD...

...AND LEAVE A CHANGELING IN ITS PLACE.
THE REAL CHILD IS RAISED ON NECTAR IN FAIRYLAND...
WHILE THE CHANGELING WITHERS IN THE CRADLE, BECOMING EVER MORE LOATHSOME TO ITS FOSTER-PARENTS.

AS BEFITTED AN EMBRYONIC MONSTEROLOGIST, I WAS A WEIRD CHILD.
1-2-3-(CLICK) 4-5-6-7 (CLICK) 8-
I MADE ENDLESS DEALS WITH THE UNIVERSE. THINGS HAD TO BE COUNTED, FORCES APPEASED.
FOR A YEAR, WHEN I WAS SIX OR SEVEN, I ALWAYS CARRIED BINOCULARS.
Ha ha binocular spastic!
6
... little girls fighting like savages!
Frances, put your arm down properly. Now.
I COULDN'T PUT IT DOWN. MY LEFT ARM PROVIDED SEATING FOR TWO IMAGINARY FAIRIES, WHO WOULD DIE IF IT WAS REMOVED.
FEY AND MENTAL THOUGH I WAS, I DO REMEMBER THIS:
01-903-7777
ACME
&CARRY
ACME
ONE DAY AT THE SHOPS WITH MUM...

EMPIRE TEA
6d LB.
OX
FREE BOBBY SANDS
IRA CUNTS
YOUR SOARAWAY
EMPIRE TEA
6d
TO TRAI
THE WORLD WAS SUDDENLY PLUNGED INTO THE 1920s (I KNEW IT FROM "LAUREL AND HARDY"). BENEATH MY FEET, I HEARD A TRAIN.
WHEN I WAS ELEVEN WE DID A LOCAL HISTORY PROJECT, AND I FOUND OUT THAT THERE WAS INDEED A TRAIN LINE RUNNING BY THAT PLACE.
OUR WORK
IT HAD BEEN SHUT FOR SIXTY YEARS.

EXPERIENCING A TIME-WARP PREPARED ME NICELY FOR LIVING WITH NANA;
SPAM
CORN CRISP

THE SEVENTY-YEAR-OLD GLAMOURPUSS WHO RECKONS SHE'S DORIS DAY.

EXCEPT DORIS DAY DOESN'T BREAKFAST ON ROTHMANS AND TIO PÉPE, AND DOESN'T THINK THAT FLAPPING ROLLS OF SKIN FORCED INTO AN ANCIENT WASPIE CORSET = A FIGURE LIKE BETTY GRABLE'S.

I SHOULD REPORT HER TO SOCIAL SERVICES FOR MAKING ME DO THE LACES UP. I'M SURE IT QUALIFIES AS SOME SORT OF PRIMAL SCENE.

Alright, Slim, whip crack-away. You'll miss assembly.
GOD! They don't have assembly at sixth-form college.

Is it your 'O' Levels you're taking now, then?
It's GCSEs – and no, I finished them. 'A' levels now. I'm a big girl.
'Ere y'are. I've made you a packed lunch
Ooh, thanks- is it Spam? Or bloater paste? I thought that was rationed.
Marge with hundreds and thousands. Your mum's favourite.
HUNDREDS AND THOUSANDS?!?
87
Bye
NO HAWKERS OR TRADERS
THE WOMAN IS A MENACE.

alright? Lovely out innit
alright? yeah.
87
KERRI IS A SLAG
NF
chicken
chicken
YEAH. REALLY, REALLY GORGEOUS.
AT LEAST THE CANNIBAL PIGEONS ARE HAPPY.
chicken

PERHAPS I'M UNDER A SPELL:
THE REAL ME HAS BEEN SPIRITED AWAY TO FAERIE...
TICKETS AND INFORMATION
UNDERGROUND
...AND I AM JUST THE CHANGELING...
Westbound Platfor
...WITHERING AMONGST THE FRIED CHICKEN BOXES.

I KIND OF LIED TO NANA.
IT'S THE SUMMER HOLIDAYS, AND THERE AREN'T ANY 'A' LEVEL CLASSES FOR ANOTHER WEEK.
I'M SUPPOSED TO GET THE RESULTS FOR MY RETAKES.
ASH WOODS
COLLEGE OF FURTHER EDUCATION
OH SHIT, I CAN'T FACE IT TODAY. I'LL GO AND SEE ALEX.

THE KAPPA

ALL JAPANESE CHILDREN KNOW TO BEWARE THE KAPPA. A RIVER SPIRIT WITH THE BODY OF A TURTLE, HE IS A BAWDY MISCHIEF-MAKER. HE IS FAMOUS FOR FARTING AND LOOKING UP PEOPLE'S SKIRTS...
BUT ALSO FOR DROWNING AND DEVOURING CHILDREN & ANIMALS.
HE LIVES IN LAKES, PONDS & RIVERS WHEREVER HUMANS SETTLE.

HIS ONE WEAKNESS IS HIS COMPULSIVE SENSE OF PROPRIETY. SO IF YOU MEET A KAPPA, GREET HIM BY NAME AND BOW POLITELY.
はじめまして、よろしくおねがいします。
きけん ちかづくな！
WHEN HE BOWS BACK, HE EMPTIES A SHALLOW HOLLOW ON THE CROWN OF HIS HEAD. THIS RENDERS HIM IMMOBILE; PARALYSED.
YOU CAN RESTORE LIFE TO THE KAPPA BY REFILLING IT FOR HIM, AT WHICH POINT HE BECOMES YOUR SERVANT.

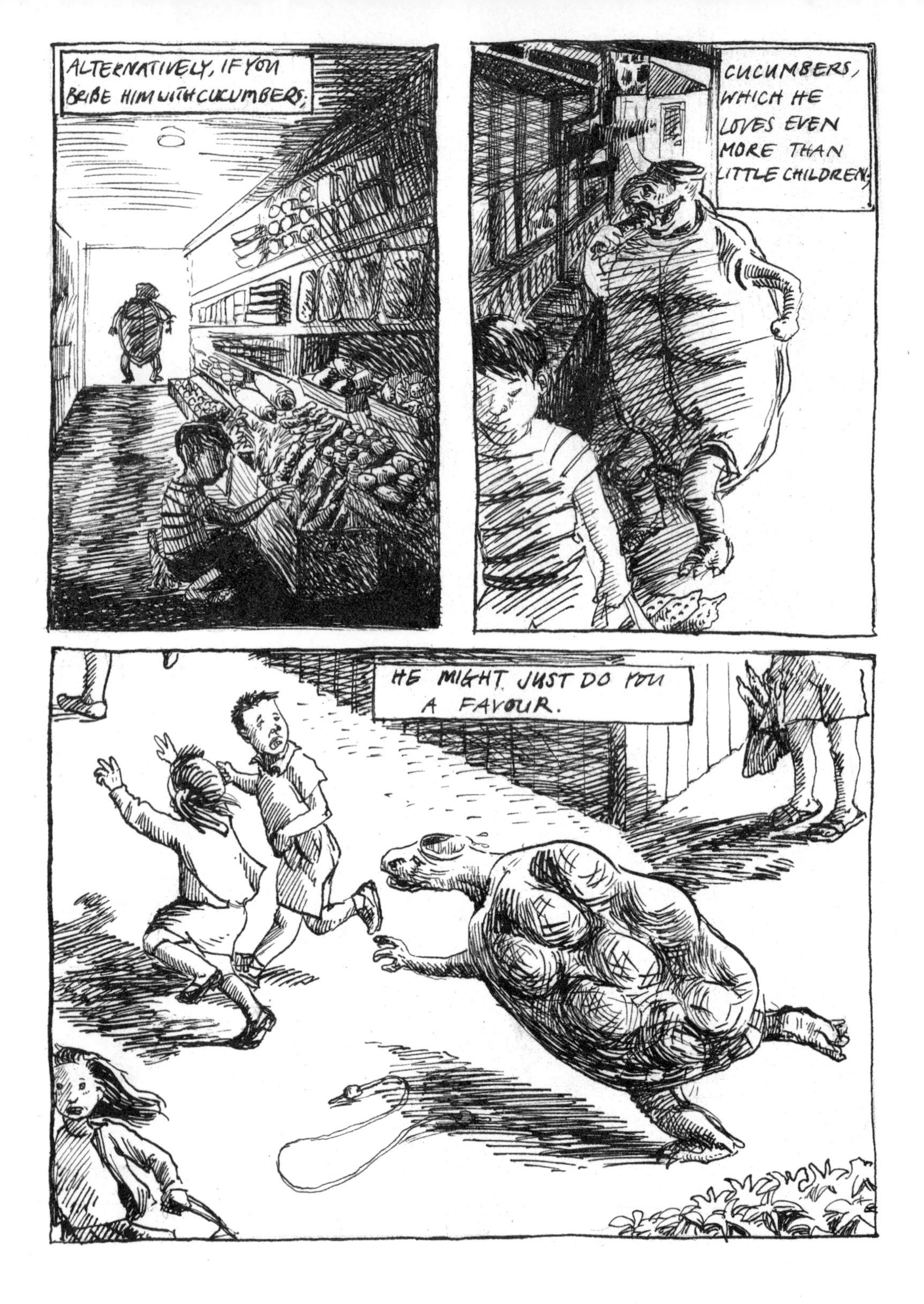
ALTERNATIVELY, IF YOU BRIBE HIM WITH CUCUMBERS,
CUCUMBERS, WHICH HE LOVES EVEN MORE THAN LITTLE CHILDREN,
HE MIGHT JUST DO YOU A FAVOUR.

AH, SUBURBIA – MY LONG-LOST HOMELAND!
SO MANY ANIMALS EVERYWHERE! NOBODY HAS PETS WHERE WE LIVE NOW. JUST INFESTATIONS.

WOLSEY
ROAD
OUR OLD ROAD...
NOPE. NOT GOING THERE.
IT'S BEEN
SIXTEEN MONTHS.
N909CBM
LEOPOLD
AVENUE

RUN LIKE THE WIND, BITCH!
DEATH'LL GET YOU
IN THE END.

OH, PLEASE BE IN, ALEX.
Stay away! There's nothing for you in here!
Hee! You're such a freak
Frankie! Listen, will you teach my daughter to be a lady?
Yeah, ok. We'll talk about nothing but netball and wedding dresses, I promise.
So-any news of your results?
Oh, they're not out yet
yeah, right
SWIFT CHANGE OF SUBJECT NEEDED..

Why do Jews always have the best biscuits?
We need the sugar to fuel our sinister manipulation of the world order. And we're not stingy yocks like your nan.
Ha ha ha ha ha!
Girls - really.
CHANGE OF SUBJECT SUCCESSFULLY IMPLEMENTED.
What shall we do? Do you want to watch 'Carrie'?
Yuk. No way.
Nah.. Got a pirate of 'Texas Chainsaw Massacre' -
These horrible films! I wash my hands of you both!

Oi! madam, don't drink all my Diet Coke, please.

Come on then, Fran, let's just have a fag and go out.

Can I have one of yours? I gave up on Sunday but it's totally boring.

Yeah — Mum? Can we have this?

Ok, as long as you don't draw on it. I save them up for Daddy's waiting-room.

Yes, promise.

Take some snacks up with you

Ok

LOADED LIKE A FREIGHT TRAIN FLYIN' LIKE AN AEROPLANE

I love your mum

Yeah, she's alright

Carrie
NIGHT
Can I put something else on? I don't feel ironic enough for Guns 'n' Roses
READY TO CRASH AN-
clunk
Do what you like. God! Why does my mother read this shit?
MY FRIENDS - THEY'RE IN MY HEAD
Give me your nail file - I need to violate Anthea Turner
No! Let me do this bitch over first
WS US
R NEW
ESHIRE
E NEST
AND ENGAND
VE PRESENT
DAUGHTER
EAUJOLAIS-
YLANNAH
ERVIEW: BIFFY FUCK-MUFF
Kill me now
CUNT
"She'll get a boob-job for laughs Steve, abo
"Motherhood is a daily blessing," gushes Sarah-Jane

"I'M MAKING THE MOST OF THE TIME I'V GOT LEFT" –
BRAVE TIFFANY SHOWS US AROUND HER LOVELY HOME
"Birdsong is a ola blessing," whisp
tick
tick
tick
tick
tick
tick
tick
tick
tick
tick
tick
tick
BOOKS OF BLOO
carrie
NIGHTMAR ON ELM STRE
Alex? Can I turn your clock off?
No, it doesn—
tick
tick

LIGHT MY CANDLE THAT'S OK 'CAUSE I FOUND GOD YEAAH

Fran? Are you OK?

Something... there's just this... like a kind of —ug- ohh. Sorry.

I GET THIS FEELING SOMETIMES

YEEAAHH YEAAHHH YEAAAHHH

urrrgghhh

LIKE IN MY GCSE EXAMS, THE FIRST TIME ROUND. EVERYTHING GOES VERY SLOW AND FLOATING.

40°

a

b

sin

x

c

x(2-1

8y

∠

cos

(+ or –)

5,7,7,7,10,11,

SOMETIMES MY TEETH FEEL REALLY BIG, AND MY FACE DOES TOO. I CAN'T BELIEVE NO ONE ELSE CAN SEE IT.

THEN – AND THIS IS AWFUL – EVERYTHING GOES FIZZY AND BUZZING, MY EYES SEE STARS AND I THINK I'M GOING TO STOP BREATHING.
ONCE, IT HAPPENED ON THE BUS.
Christmas MAGIC at DEBENHA
You all right there, darling?
She's on drugs. It's disgusting.
YOU CAN KIND OF SEE YOURSELF FROM OUTSIDE.
huh huh
ONE THING CAN USUALLY STOP THE FEELING IN ITS TRACKS.
NAMING MONSTERS.

IT'S ALL ABOUT CONTROL. IF YOU CAN NAME IT— DESCRIBE ITS HABITS— KNOW ITS WEAK SPOTS— IT CAN'T HAVE YOU.

GIRLS CHAMPION UNDER 14
Poor Fran. Let's go and get stoned on the golf course.
Fear of Flying Erica Jong
Movie monsters
J.D. Salinger The Catcher in the Rye
THE SHINING
Virginia Woolf Mrs. Dalloway
ANGELA CARTER The Magic Toyshop
Beauty Tips for Girls
The Secret Diary of Adrian Mole aged 13 3/4 The Growing Pains of Adrian Mole Sue Townsend
ENCYCLOPAEDIA OF THE HORROR FILM
Jackie FOR GIRLS ANNUAL 1987
PEANUTS
THE BEANO BOOK 1984
MOVIE PSYCHOS AND MADMEN

LITTLE BABY
GONNA COME WITH ME
IF YOU DON'T COME
IF YOU DON'T
COME
Blyton
by
IF YOU DON'T
COME
YOU'LL DIIE
ALOOONE
See you Mum
We're just going
for a coffee
Ok, bye ladies.
Have fun.
Take care, Fran
Bye
thanks

THE BLACK DOG
NEVER TALK TO A BLACK DOG: IT IS LIABLE TO TALK BACK.
Madam?

THERE ARE SEVERAL TYPES OF BLACK DOG. THE FIRST IS THE SHAPE-SHIFTING TYPE. IT IS KNOWN BY MANY NAMES...
BLACK SHUCK, BARGHEST, GYTRASH, PADFOOT, SKRIKER, HOOTER, KLUDDE. IT CAN APPEAR AS A HEADLESS CALF; A BALL OF MARSH-FIRE; A SNOW-WHITE DONKEY; A WINDING SHEET... IT IS AN ILL-OMENED THING, SOME SAY DEMONIC.
SOME BLACK DOGS ARE THE GUARDIANS OF SACRED SITES—STANDING STONES, CHURCHYARDS, THE LONG-FORGOTTEN INTERSECTIONS OF LEY LINES.
OTHERS SEEM TO BE THE GHOSTS OF REAL DOGS, OR OF HUMANS. THIS TYPE CAN BE BENIGN; PROTECTIVE, EVEN. HOWEVER —

IF, ONE LONELY MIDNIGHT,
ON A COUNTRY ROAD,
YOU WERE TO HEAR FOOTSTEPS BEHIND YOU-
-IF YOU WERE TO FEEL HOT ANIMAL BREATH AT YOUR HEELS-
TO TURN AROUND WOULD SEAL YOUR DOOM: FOR A BLACK DOG, ONCE ACKNOWLEDGED,
MEANS CERTAIN DEATH.

Are you really worried about your results?
I don't know... yes. If they're crap I'm fucked. And if they're good, it means...
It means you're really clever and brilliant. Which you are.
... it means this bit's finished and I've got to, I don't know, move on...
... to... something.
You can always join me on my hair & beauty course. It's deeply intellectually stimulating. There's just so much to learn about follicles and toner!

You got registration tomorrow, haven't you? Are you dreading it?

PRIVATE PROPERTY

TRESPASSERS WILL BE PROSECUTED

Nah. It's a total means to an end. It'll get me on a proper theatrical one next year...

Urgh, dog shit! Sorry

Then you can get a job doing all burns victims on 'Casualty'

Yeah! And then the proper horror stuff –

– Imagine if I could invent another Pinhead! Or Freddy Krueger!

Aah. You're every mother's dream, Alex.

I know.

Wow! what are those purple things?
Er.. rose-bay willowherb.
TRESP
WILL BE
Yeah. Nana calls it fireweed – it grows out of ashes. There was loads after the Blitz.
Mm-hmm.
Means summer's nearly over
"The summer of ninety-three." Why can't we have important summers, like in "The Wonder Years"?

Because we're not on telly? Plus we're English –
"I wasn't a girl — and I wasn't quite a woman" –
"But that summer, my anorak had got quite a bit tighter round the arms"!
Ha ha! But it'd be good if shit stuff that happened really was character-building, wouldn't it?
Yup.

I wish our lives had, you know, a soundtrack.

Yeah – you'd know what to *feel* about stuff.

Even drinking cider round the back of Argos would look all noble and cinematic

When you got sad, your life would always sound like a shit soft metal ballad. Or Boyz II Men...

What's *your* theme music?

God. Probably some Pixies. The way they start calm... but always end up mental

Do you remember at primary school that game where you spun round and —

— and pretended to see into the future!

I was going to marry David Hasselhoff, drive a pale blue Fiesta and be a gymnast!

Haha! Nice.

Can you imagine really being grown up, though?

Yeah, 'course. It's just a few years' time from now. I'll be a make-up artist. Be married... or in a nurturing long-term partnership with Slash.

I can't. I can't imagine the future. It's like — a big, white wall.

rrrrgh

huh huh

Alex – what was that noise?

Dunno – an American werewolf?

Don't, it's not funny

Promise me you won't turn around?

OK

huh huh

SHEBA! DOWN!
good girl
Fucking hell!
You do know this is private property, girls- you're trespassing.
Yeah, did you know PROPERTY IS THEFT, capitalist golf bastards?
So sorry, sir, we got a bit lost.

You can stop staring now if you want, pervert
bitches
HA HA HA HA HA HA HA
What time's it?
Five, I think - Why - have you got to go and meet Needle-Dick the Bug Fucker?
Yeah - oi! Don't call him that!
Well, Ok. As long as he takes his beret off when you do it - And phone me if you do...
Yeah, allright... and thanks for the spliff

Love you
Love you too
BY NEEDLE-DICK, I THINK SHE MEANS SAM. SAM IS MY "BOYFRIEND". (I DON'T KNOW WHY I HAVE TO SAY THAT IN QUOTATION MARKS.)
HE IS VERY POSH AND ALEX THINKS HE IS PRETENTIOUS BUT I AM REALLY IN LOVE WITH HIM. WE HAVEN'T DONE IT YET BUT I AM ALWAYS TRYING TO GET HIM TO.
87

THE GOLEM
A GOLEM IS A CREATURE BUILT OF CLAY . . .

...MADE ANIMATE THROUGH ECSTATIC RITUAL BY A MAN OF GOD.
ON ITS FOREHEAD ARE CARVED THE LETTERS
MEANING TRUTH, OR THE REAL... EMET.
ONE SUCH CREATURE WAS MADE BY RABBI LOEW BEN BEZALEL IN PRAGUE...
...TO DEFEND HIS GHETTO AGAINST ANTI-SEMITIC ATTACKS.

BUT AS THE CREATURE LIVED, IT GREW AND BECAME VIOLENT — KILLING GENTILES AND TURNING AGAINST THE RABBI.
HE REMOVED THE ALEPH FROM ITS BROW, TURNING 'EMET' INTO 'MET'; 'DEAD'!
THUS, THE GOLEM WAS DESTROYED.

OK
Come in, I'm just reading my book. How was school?
Nana? Do you want anything from the Spar shop?
No thank you, darling. You out tonight?
Yeah. Sam. Be back late.

SPAR
WOOD'S PIES EELS MASH
LIQUOR
Shazia
CLOSED
SPAR
Hello, dear
Hi, Mrs Philpott
Are you going out, then?
Not yet, just going for some cigarettes

I can't move, you know, dear. My leg's very badly.
Would you be able to walk me to church for the seven o'clock service?
Church? Erm... all right.
Where are we going then? St. Michael's?
Oh no, I'm with the Spiritualists round the corner.

What, really? Like, do people really come back and tell you stuff from the afterlife?
Well yes, sometimes I think they do. And it's an outing. You can get a coffee and that
I don't think I want to hear about what it's like being a spirit. Do I have to come in?
SPIRITUALIST
ASSOCIATION
– a round of applause for our guest medium, Michael Reid!
Just help me sit down, love
Sh! Sit down!
Shh!
SHIT.

My love and greetings to you all, those on Earth and those in Spirit. Now – ah, it's an elderly gentleman –
– says he wants to talk to you, pet –
?
– Jim? James? He liked a laugh and a joke, didn't he... now he's showing me a mug, or a cup –

I'm getting Camp coffee – aye, that's a blast from the past – Camp coffee and a Morris Minor?

Nope

He says the money's in the metal teapot.

Nana's stash of Rothmans is in the teapot!

Shush, dear

This gentleman didn't suffer fools, pet. He's saying – no! He's saying "Mind your Ps and Qs!"

Is that something you can take?

Obviously not.

I'm getting a smell-
oh - a smell of -
burning flesh!
Who burnt to death?

Erm... nobody?

What you cannot take will come.

Amazing, Michael!

Thanks, Wendy

Now, these voices from Spirit can leave Michael depleted - and he's already given so much...

... so while he recovers his spiritual energy, I'd like to remind you of this week's raffle. Just 20p can win you...
... a basket of miniature guest soaps, lots of other goodies...
... and another unique dolly from Ethel. Thank you, Ethel.
So as you can see we're got...
Sh!

I'm ready again, wendy - if you could just step aside and make room for another visitor from Spirit - Yes. Yes, mate. I'm here for you.

I'm getting a young man in army uniform... little fella, about five-six -

Ooh! It's my Clark!

Lovely hair – lovely dark curls
yes!
Red hair!

Come into the light, Clark, mate. Ah aye, I can see – a real copperknob.
He was lost in France, pet. 1941, 1942...

1943! Is he happy? Can you tell?
Oh, Ivy!

He's showing me a little dog – can you take a Jack Russell?
Well – we had a cocker spaniel when we was littl'uns...

Aye, that'll be it.
He says he'll always love his Ivy, his little wifie, he says ...
Eh? He was my brother!
As close as husband and wife, maybe were yous, pet?
Tssk! What is he chatting about?
He was my brother! I never been...
I am just a channel for what comes through from Spirit. Oh – he says not to worry about that terrible thing you did –
Eh? I don't know –
– or will do. What you cannot take will come. Thank you.

Don't take on so, darling

I thought it was him Annie

I know... stupid boy

He's really upset that old - that lady

You get an eye for the fakes, dear. But you can't throw the baby out with the bathwater.

I'm gonna go, will you be OK?

Sit down!

Oh yes, Annie and Ivy'll see me back indoors.

FUCKING HELL.

THE INCUBUS

AN INCUBUS IS A DEMON...
WHO STEALS THE SEMINAL FLUID OF SLUMBERING MEN...
MOUNTS THE LOINS OF SOME WOMAN AS SHE TOO IS ASLEEP...

AND IMPREGNATES HER WITH IT.
OTHER CULTURES HAVE THEIR INCUBI:
IN HUNGARY, THE LIDÉRC IS A SATANIC LOVER WHO COMES TO SINGLE WOMEN.
IT APPEARS AS A FIRE, OR MORE PROSAICALLY, AS A FEATHERLESS CHICKEN.
IN AMAZONIAN BRAZIL, UNWANTED PREGNANCIES AND "MYSTERIOUS" DISAPPEARANCES ARE TRADITIONALLY BLAMED ON THE BOTO, WHICH APPEARS IN THE GUISE OF A BEAUTIFUL YOUNG MAN AND DEPARTS BY DAYLIGHT, A BLITHE UNEARTHLY CREATURE LIKE A DOLPHIN.
WHEREVER IT COMES TO YOU, REGULAR ENCOUNTERS WITH AN INCUBUS WILL LEAD TO FAILING HEALTH, MADNESS OR EVEN DEATH.

derbra
St Paul's cathedral
SAUNA
I HOPE SAM'S UP FOR A PINT... OR FOUR.
WHERE IS HE?
93
TWO JAYS
MISSISSIPPI CHICKEN
OH. THERE.

OH GOD, HE'S WEARING ONE OF HIS WEIRD 'ENSEMBLES'.
Alright? You're looking very frilly.
Hmm. Any news of the exams?
No —

I HOPE WE DON'T SEE ANYONE I KNOW.
UNDERGROUN
NO POLL TAX
MISSING
I reckon it'll be an 'A' for English and loads of 'U's. I was on acid in all the others.*
Can we go to the pub?
Sure. This looks like a comfortingly petit-bourgeois little hostelry
* a lie

YOUNG'S
Hey, look at cravat man — he's like someone out of Iris Murdoch. Do you reckon he's drinking 'perry and ginger wine, garnished with a celery stalk'? Or 'India Pale Ale and milk with two ice cubes'
WHY DO I NEED TO IMPRESS SAM? I'M SO TEDIOUS.
Shh! Don't talk. I simply must draw you like that...
I love it that you like me for my mind...
YUP. HE THINKS SO TOO.

Sam?
Shhh
Am I your muse?
No, I don't think I've met her yet
!!

Is it that Sloane, Felicity?
No.
Or her slag sister?
No.
Georgina? I bet it's Georgina
This is getting rather boring
NOW HE'S ACTUALLY SAID IT.

Quick, let's go - I want to look at you in Nature before the sun goes down completely.
What? I've still got half a pint! And there isn't any nature.

GARDEN→
I just meant the beer garden, silly girl! You are a creature of the earth and fresh air...
Fuck's sake
Shall I roll up my sleeves and start digging, then? You can exercise your 'droit du seigneur' and rape me in the mangel-wurzels

OK, HE MAY BE PRETENTIOUS, BUT I'LL NEVER PULL ANYONE THIS GOOD-LOOKING EVER AGAIN.
Hey; come in for a joint. There aren't any turds or syringes, it's lovely

Welcome to the Magic Faraway Tree! You can be Dame Spank

oof

OBVIOUSLY I'M FANNY.

I BET WE LOOK REALLY SEXY. IF WE WERE IN A FILM IT WOULD BE A REALLY GOOD KISSING SCENE.

Christ I'm hard. suck my cock.

AAARGGGHHH!

OH GOD, WHAT DID ALEX SAY AGAIN? DO YOU DO IT LIKE THIS?

OR THIS?
OH. RIGHT.
aah
urp
aak
Whoah, baby Yeaaah.
gllp
WELL, A RITE OF PASSAGE TICKED OFF THE LIST, I SUPPOSE!

How was my cock? Did you take it all down?
snigger
WHAT? I'VE TURNED SAM INTO SOME OUT-OF-CONTROL PORNO TWAT!
Come here, my little cockney sparrow
What the fuck are you on about? I'm as middle-class as you are! Nearly.
D'you reckon you're on, like, posho safari or something? Coming round here...?
Look, it's different for a man. I was properly scared coming out of the Tube.
Why?
These Indian boys gave me a really dirty look, you know.
Bangladeshi. Racist.
It's 9.30: I'd better get going see you later.
Thanks for the formative sexual experience. And watch out for scary poor people.

CHILDREN ONLY
SOD

THE BANNIK
IN THE VAST AND FROZEN COUNTRY OF THE NORTH AND IN THE ENDLESS CENTRAL FORESTS, THE SLAVONIC PEOPLE KNEW THE WORLD TO BE FULL OF SPIRITS, WHO SHARED THEIR HUMAN SPACES — SOMETIMES UNSEEN, SOMETIMES NOT.
THERE WAS A SMALL DOMESTIC GOD OR TUTELARY SPIRIT CALLED THE DOMOVOI, WHO WEPT BEFORE A DEATH IN THE FAMILY.
OTHER AREAS OF THE HOMESTEAD HAD THEIR OCCUPANTS — THE DVOROVOI LIVED IN THE YARD (AND LOATHED ALL WHITE ANIMALS) —
— AND THE OVINNIK LIVED IN THE BARN AND HAD THE ASPECT OF A HUGE, DISHEVELLED BLACK CAT.

THE BANNIK LIVED IN THE BATH-HOUSE. THREE OUT OF EVERY FOUR BATHS DRAWN, HE WOULD ALLOW FOR HUMANS, BUT THE FOURTH WAS HIS OWN. HE WOULD ENJOY A BATHTIME BACCHANAL WITH DEVILS AND FOREST-SPIRITS, AND SCALD ANYBODY WHO DISTURBED HIM.
THE BANNIK HAD AN ORACULAR FUNCTION AND COULD BE CALLED UPON FOR A GENERAL FORECAST:
IF YOU PRESENTED YOUR NAKED BACK TO THE BATHHOUSE DOOR AND HE CARESSED IT WITH THE PALM OF HIS HAND, THE OUTLOOK WAS ROSY.
BUT IF HE STRUCK YOU WITH HIS CLAWS, BAD TIMES WERE COMING.

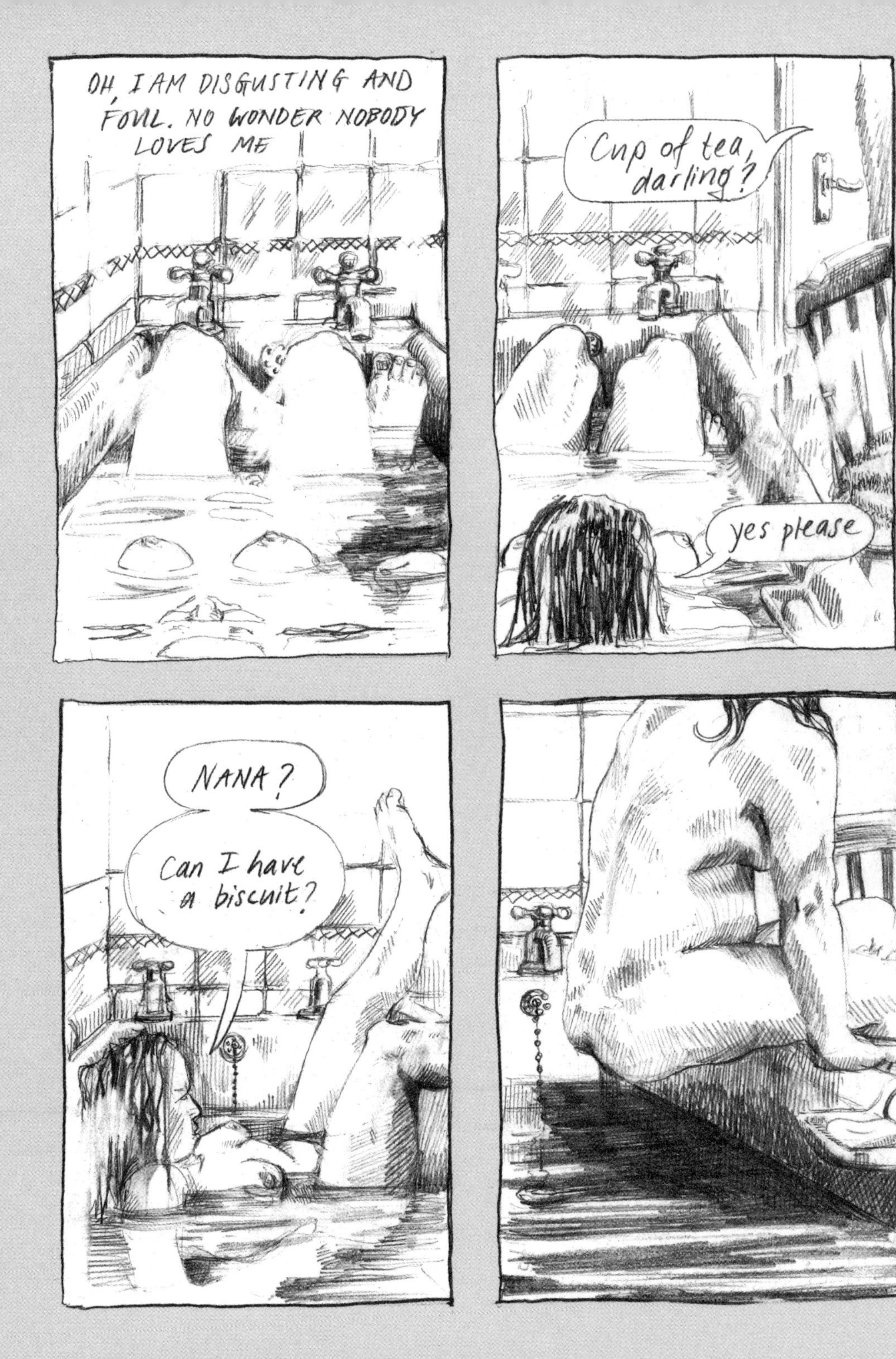
OH, I AM DISGUSTING AND FOUL. NO WONDER NOBODY LOVES ME
Cup of tea, darling?
yes please
NANA?
Can I have a biscuit?

Frances! Tea!
snff
coming.

Sit up straight, darling. You'll ruin your figure.
I haven't got a figure, I'm a massive giant blob.
Aww, you're the spit of your mum at your age...

She was lovely...

"...lovely big girl; all that free orange juice on the NHS."

She was ever so clever, just like you... and such a good little actress

Acting? Really?

Oh yes! All sorts of clever things with chairs, and a funny one in a sandpit. I did like that "Mr. Cinders", though. "Spread a little ha-ppiness as you go by—" yes, that was nice

Do I look like my dad's family?
No, dear, there's none of his lot in there.
I CAN ONLY JUST REMEMBER MY DAD'S PARENTS.
THERE WAS A TALL, FUNNY GRANDAD
AND A STERN BUT CUDDLY GRANDMA.
MY VISITS WITH THEM COME BACK TO ME AS LOVELY ENID BLYTON-Y TIMES OF HIGH TEAS, AND BEETLE DRIVES, AND GAMES OF 'WOODLAND HAPPY FAMILIES.'
MRS. OWL
MOUSE PIE
I HAVEN'T SEEN THEM SINCE MUM LEFT DAD.
NEARLY TEN YEARS AGO.
I'M SUPPOSED TO BE SEEING DAD —
Tomorrow, ain't it?
BLOODY HELL, ALRIGHT, MYSTIC MEG.

He said we were going to "do" breakfast. I said we normally eat it round here, but if breakfast was willing...

Smart-Aleck.

I thought it was somewhat Ortonesque...

He's trying, darling... Here, my feet need doing. If I soak them, would you -

Ha ha! No! Get them away from me!

Hee hee! - Cut my corns!

All night, I'm going to bed. 'Night.

Night night. God bless

Are you going yet?

No, you know I don't sleep much these days. Besides, there's that Michael Caine on in a film. I'll have meself a toyboy!

I'LL LEAVE HER TO FLICK HERSELF OFF TO "ALFIE".

'night, Kurt.

HE WILL WATCH OVER ME.

huh
huh
A DREAM OF FALLING...
BUT WHY CAN'T I MOVE?
A DREADFUL DRONING IN MY EAR
AND PRESSING ON MY CHEST...

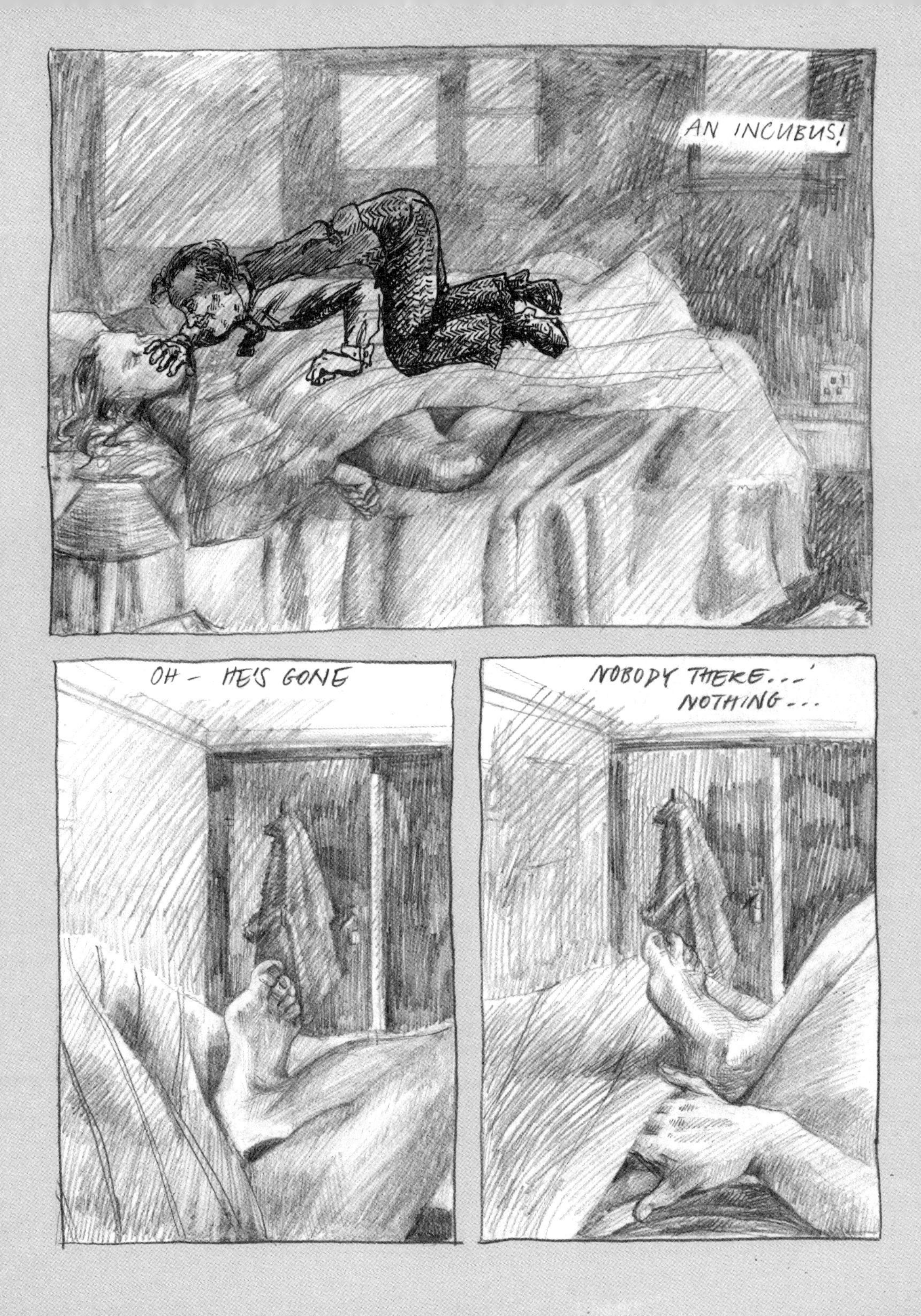
AN INCUBUS!
OH - HE'S GONE
NOBODY THERE...
NOTHING...

I AM IN THE NEVADA DESERT WITH MUM AND DAD.
THE SKY IS VERY LOW AND THERE MAY BE A NUCLEAR WAR.
WE HAVE TO GO INTO A HOTEL. IT LOOKS VERY SMALL AT FIRST
BUT INSIDE THERE IS A DINING HALL WHERE WE WILL HAVE DINNER WITH A CULT.

THE DINNER IS GOING TO BE SOUP.
THE CULT LEADER IS STING, WHO PUTS SOME BLOOD IN A CHAFING-DISH AND THEN INTO THE SOUP TUREEN.
HE CHANTS SOME WORDS IN A DEEP VOICE WHICH IS UNLIKE HIS NORMAL, REEDY ONE.
STING MAKES US EAT THE SOUP.
FIRST, WE LOSE THE ABILITY TO SPEAK.

THEN, WE FORGET WHO WE ARE RELATED TO...
...AND JUST WANDER AROUND OUTSIDE, WHERE SUDDENLY A TERRIBLE SUN IS SHINING.
I AM CHOSEN TO BE A SACRIFICE: DRUGGED AGAIN; BATHED;
AND GIVEN TO STING.

TAKE SUCK OF ME
HE SAYS.
AND I DIE.
I'M ON THE TUBE...BUT I'M DEAD. I'M DEAD. THESE ARE THE DEAD.
I'M LIKE THEM NOW.

Uxbridge
Formless Spirit
Moksha
Samsara
Kaddish
Paternoster Street
Bardo
Sheol
Infernus
Lucifer Green
Gehenna
Pandemonium
Shedim
Hades West
Abadon
Sodom
Axis Mundi
Myeloma Park
Necrosis
Nadir
Scab
King Rat
Old Bastard Street
Metastasis Park
Limbo
Sepsis
Loss
Excision
I AM ON THE SECRET TUBE LINE OF THE DEAD. A TERRIBLE FEAR PUTS ITS HANDS AROUND MY GUT...
...AND TWISTS.
THE DEAD SMILE WANLY AT ME; WELCOMING.
FRED ASTAIRE COMES AND GIVES ME A BAG.
It's your one-way ticket outta here!
HE SAYS
AND DANCES AWAY
you gotta look for it, kid!

WHAT? WHAT HAVE I GOT TO LOOK FOR?
I DON'T KNOW WHAT IT IS, BUT I FEEL AS THOUGH I'VE LOST SOMETHING EXTREMELY PRECIOUS.
THE LIGHT'S TOO BRIGHT TO SEE ANYTHING
AND SOME ANIMAL IS MAKING A HIGH, KEENING NOISE AS IF IT IS IN PAIN.
I WAKE UP. THE KEENING GOES ON. WHERE IS IT COMING FROM?
COOLLY, I OBSERVE THAT IT IS COMING
FROM ME.

THE BOGGART

A BOGGART IS SOMETHING LIKE A HOUSE BROWNIE, BUT MISCHIEVOUS, EVEN MALIGNANT.
UNLIKE A BROWNIE, IT CANNOT BE PLACATED WITH DISHES OF CREAM.
IT CONDUCTS ITSELF, LIKE A POLTERGEIST, WITH GLEEFUL MISRULE, AND WILL ATTACH ITSELF TO A FAMILY...
to let
LET
...HAPPILY FOLLOWING THEM IF THEY TRY TO MOVE AWAY.
Aye, we're flitting

MODERN FOLKLORISTS HAVE NOTED SIMILARITIES TO THE 'GREMLIN' OF THE WORLD WARS, WHICH WOULD MEDDLE WITH PLANES
Here, Cyril- this keeps on coming loose
Aah, there's a bleeding gremlin in the works!
AND CAUSE THE DEATHS OF UNLUCKY AIRMEN...
AND THERE'S DEFINITELY ONE HANGING AROUND ME.
BOVRIL
WHAT THE—

Wakey wakey, rise and sh-
SHUTUP!
Well!
Yeah, alright. Sorry.
shit
OW!
Buy Rite
CORN CRISP

NO. NO WAY DID I ACTUALLY SEE THAT.
OW! SHIT!
Tssk! Language
(BUT IT'S STILL THERE)
PLAYING GRANDMOTHER'S FOOTSTEPS; A HORRID HOPPING THING, JUST OUT OF SIGHT
87

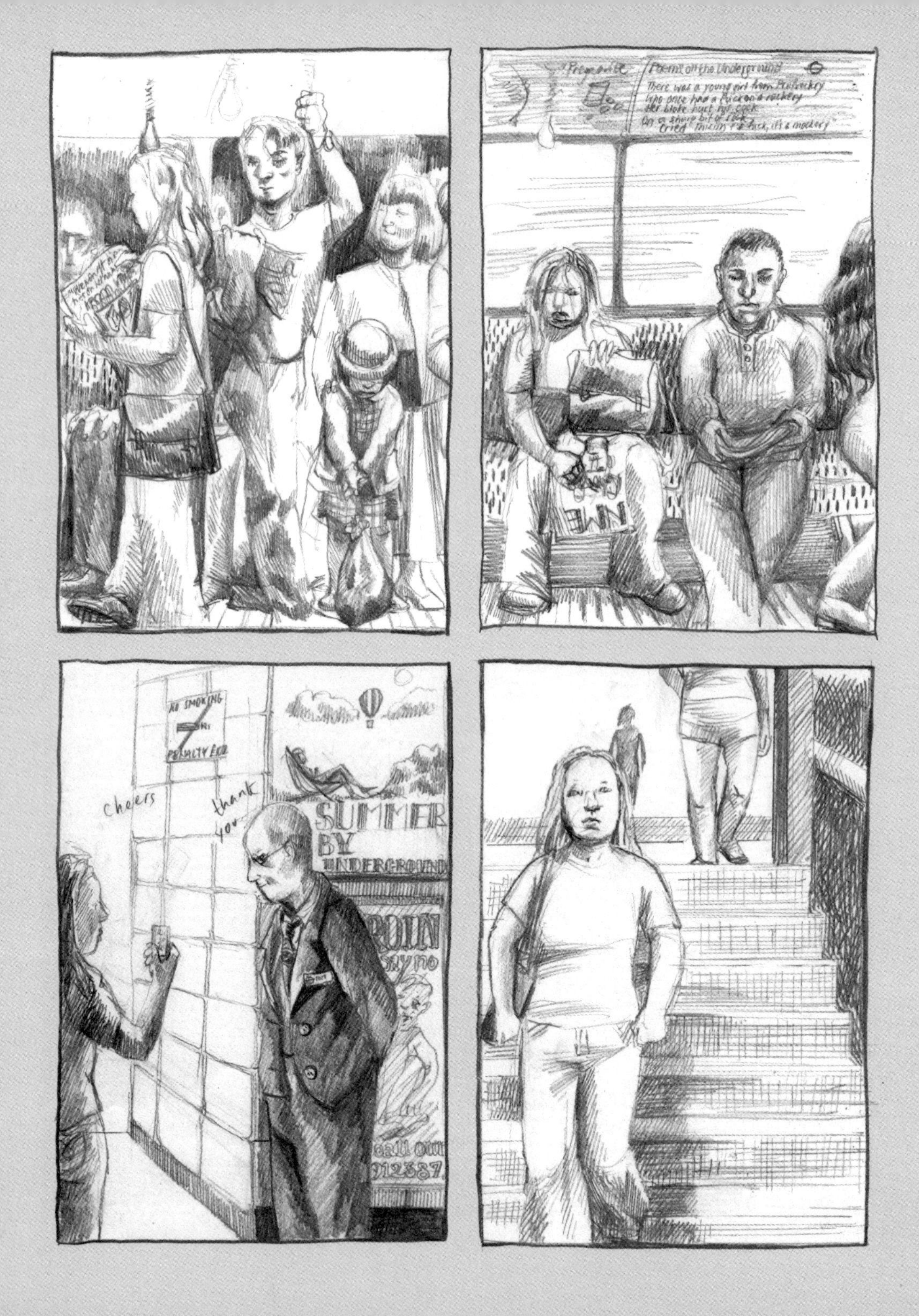
Poems on the Underground
NME
NO SMOKING
cheers
thank you
SUMMER
BY
UNDERGROUND

Let's go to that new place on the Broadway
I've already had breakfast...
Why?
...Well, I had some toast
Actually I totally burnt it

Le Deli
de Deli
du Nor
BRUNCH
MENU
What the fuck is a "brunch" anyway?
Le Deli
du Nord

A cross between breakfast and lunch
What, like cornflake sandwiches?
No, I think it's American
Hiya, what can I get you?
Hi- I'll have the smoked salmon platter, please.

Yeah, me too please, and can I have a big milky coffee as well?

Large double latte?

If that's what the kids are calling them.

Thanks

Makes a nice change from bloater paste and Carnation milk... Do you mind if I smoke?

Yes.

Do you "brunch" every day then? I'm feeling very, like, Barnardo's home in comparison.

Do you need money? You know, apart from child support —

Yeah, but I don't want any, thanks.
I was just commenting facetiously on our class disparity, despite being closely related...
I think you're exaggerating...
Tell that to my "lifestyle". And to Nana.
How is Irene?
Really really well. She's brilliant.
Two smoked salmon platters? I'll just bring your latte.
Wow

So! It's results time! Are you feeling nervous?
Nah, they're retakes so I've had twice as long as everyone else
What are you going to do next?
Probably go on the game? You can get forty shillings for the special stuff up West, I hear.
No.... 'A' Levels. English and History and stuff.
How's Angie and the erm...
Great. They're great - Look...

Jessica ... and Amber.
Jessica was five on Thursday
They're ... lovely. So sweet This one looks like you.
Ha! There's one of me! Oh my god ...
I can remember being sick on that skirt at your mum – at Grandma's house

Ha! You always used to be sick on the way back, in exactly the same place on the North Circular

Do you remember that?

God, yeah

Everything OK?

Yes thank you

Yeah lovely thanks

It's nearly 10, I'll drop you off. By the way, I rang the other night. Your nana didn't know where you were.

She doesn't usually. I do tell her sometimes but she doesn't really understand what happens once you get past Shoreditch. She thinks it's, like, fields and chicken sheds.

It doesn't seem right. No one knowing where you are.

Well, that's how it is. I can't do anything about it, can I?

I... OK. Let's get going, the traffic's bad.

MANHATTAN

Phone me when you know.
Mmm. Bye. Thanks for "brunch".

THE BRAG
A BRAG IS A SHAPE-SHIFTER, A LOCAL DEVIL OF THE NORTH COUNTRY. A RELATION OF THE PUCCAS AND KELPIES OF IRELAND AND SCOTLAND, IT WILL TAKE ON THE SHAPE OF SOMETHING FAMILIAR IN ORDER TO MISLEAD-AND INJURE- THE UNWARY. IT OFTEN APPEARS LIKE A HORSE...

... BUT CAN ALSO BECOME A CALF, WEARING A WHITE KERCHIEF; ...
... A NAKED MAN WITHOUT A HEAD; ...
FOUR MEN, HOLDING A WHITE SHEET.
IT WAS SAID TO HAVE TAKEN CHILDREN AWAY AND DROWNED THEM, IN DEEP AND WATERY PLACES.

RECEPTION
CUNT
OH GOD. EVERYONE'S BACK ALREADY.

Phil Collins No Jacket Required
Phil Collins Tour 1986
No Jacket Required
A-lex! I can't believe you just blanked your boyfriend
hee hee!
Oh my God, there's Crap Slash
Alright? Good holiday?
Hi Ben
Yeah man, good times... played a gig at Camden Palace...
Yeah, just the usual girly crap- drug rape, flute lessons... you?
Cool
... laters
"Laters"

'Laters'! You totally fancy him

Ahem! You mean you do!

Yeah I know, but only in a fantasy way

You know - I'd think about Crap Slash - I mean Ben - if I was having a you-know-what... but he only really goes for weird guitar girls like Lucy.

What's the difference, I'd like to know?

Why wouldn't you want to go out with him though?

Oh God, he's such a poser! Talking of which, how's Sam?

Shit. Don't wanna talk about it.

Oh. Sorry.

S'alright.

Well - you're only a guitar and a nose-ring away from being Crap Slash's dream girl!

Ha ha. I don't want everyone to know I feel alienated just by *looking* at me.

WHY AM I LIKE THIS?
I'M NOT A...
criminal
kook
jock
brain
prom queen
OR EVEN ONE OF ASHWOODS SIXTH FORM'S MORE NOTABLE FREAKS...
LIKE DAVID PLANTER, WHO CLAIMS HE'S ON PROBATION FOR TWOCKING (SOMETIMES IT'S FOR ARSON)...
EMPTY EYES
PRISON TATTOO DONE IN A GEOGRAPHY LESSON
BRIEFCASE HIS MUM BOUGHT FOR HIM
HE ISN'T, BUT HE'S STILL SCARY.
OR LUCY, WITH HER OSTENTATIOUS SELF-HARM & TIRESOME RIOT GRRL SCHTICK...
'SHOCKING' T-SHIRT.
(I AM ACTUALLY A BIT IMPRESSED)
CUNT
PINK 'SOBRANIE COCKTAIL' FAG
HUGGY BEAR
PARATROOPER BOOTS LIBERATED FROM THE MILITARY-INDUSTRIAL FASCISTS VIA CAMDEN MARKET
SHIT PSEUDO-FEMINIST BAND WORSHIP
OR THE WEIRDEST OF ALL...
SEAN 'MICKEY J.' ASTON,
CLIP-ON JHERI CURL HAIRPIECE
MADE FOR HIM BY SYMPATHETIC FASHION STUDENT
GOD KNOWS WHAT HORRORS MADE HIM LIKE THIS...
STANDARD WITNESS-WEAR!
(WELL, ACTUALLY, HE TOLD ME – HE'S GAY, BUT HIS MUM'S A JEHOVAH'S WITNESS: HE COMES TO COLLEGE IN A TIE, THEN CHANGES IN THE BOGS)

EVEN SO, I'M NOT NORMAL...
Whoops-sorry! Haha
Ouch
NORMAL PEOPLE CAN SMELL IT ON ME —A SORT OF METAPHYSICAL B.O.
Chantal! Hiya!
Aleex! Darling
Hi, Fran.
Hi, Caz.
Good holiday, yeah?
mwa
Yeah, we went to Provence. It was really nice.
Really? I did Tel Aviv. Looking forward to term?
Snap for France! Daddy got us rooms at 'le George Cinq' —sooo stunning!
What about you, Fran?
Oh. Nothing really.
Oh my God, I totally forgot. Sorry.
Yup.

Fran!
One minute, OK?
I can't believe your tutor looks like Special Agent Dale Cooper and mine looks like Pat Butcher! Bitch.
ASH GROVE
Frances,
Please be at College
Appointment with
I can't believe you want to stroke his rancid ponytail. Oh God, Alex. Will it be all right?
So, great news, huh? Sit down, sit down.
Great what?
Your GCSE retakes results, of course.
I haven't_
Weren't you here yesterday?
Oh. No, I—
Didn't you want to know what you'd got?
NO, NOT REALLY.

Fuck! (sorry..)

ha ha

BRISTOW, Frances Esme

SE Art and Design	A (a)
nglish (Language)	A (a)
nglish (Literature)	A (a)
French	A (a)
Geography	B (b)
History	A (a)
Latin	C (c)
Mathematics	A (a)
eligious Studies	A (a)

Your – ah – grandma'll be chuffed, huh?

Mm-hm

YEAH, RIGHT.

AS MIDDLE-CLASS PARENTS THROUGHOUT THE LAND REWARD THEIR CLEVER DARLINGS...

Thanks, Mummy! Thanks, Daddy!

You can drive it to Oxford, eh?

...NANA WILL REMAIN DOWN-TO-EARTH.

GCS-what? They're after young blood down the bolt factory, my girl

MUM WOULD BE SO—

Well done, darling
-yes.
OH GOD. I FELT HER ARMS WRAP AROUND ME.
So! Seven 'A's! Only 'A' Levels to go now-
I FELT HER ARMS AROUND ME
-and the world's your oyster
well done, darling
I FELT HER ARMS
Just to dangle the carrot a bit: I thought you might enjoy UEA. Very creative atmos- Hello? Earth to Fran?
HER ARMS

HER _
Erm... have you got any thoughts on the future?
On thhgg..
urghhh
Oh. Oh dear. Erm...

Alex, is it? Can you come in here a minute?

She - er, do you think you could...

It's OK

She did really well in her exams...

Come on, Fran. Come on, baby.

Fucking men don't know anything. Stay there, I'll ring your nan.

I think so...
...yeah, thanks, I'll tell her...
...OK bye, Rene.
...You too.

She's not going out anywhere. Are you OK to get the train?

yeah. yeah

I know I don't really understand but I love you.

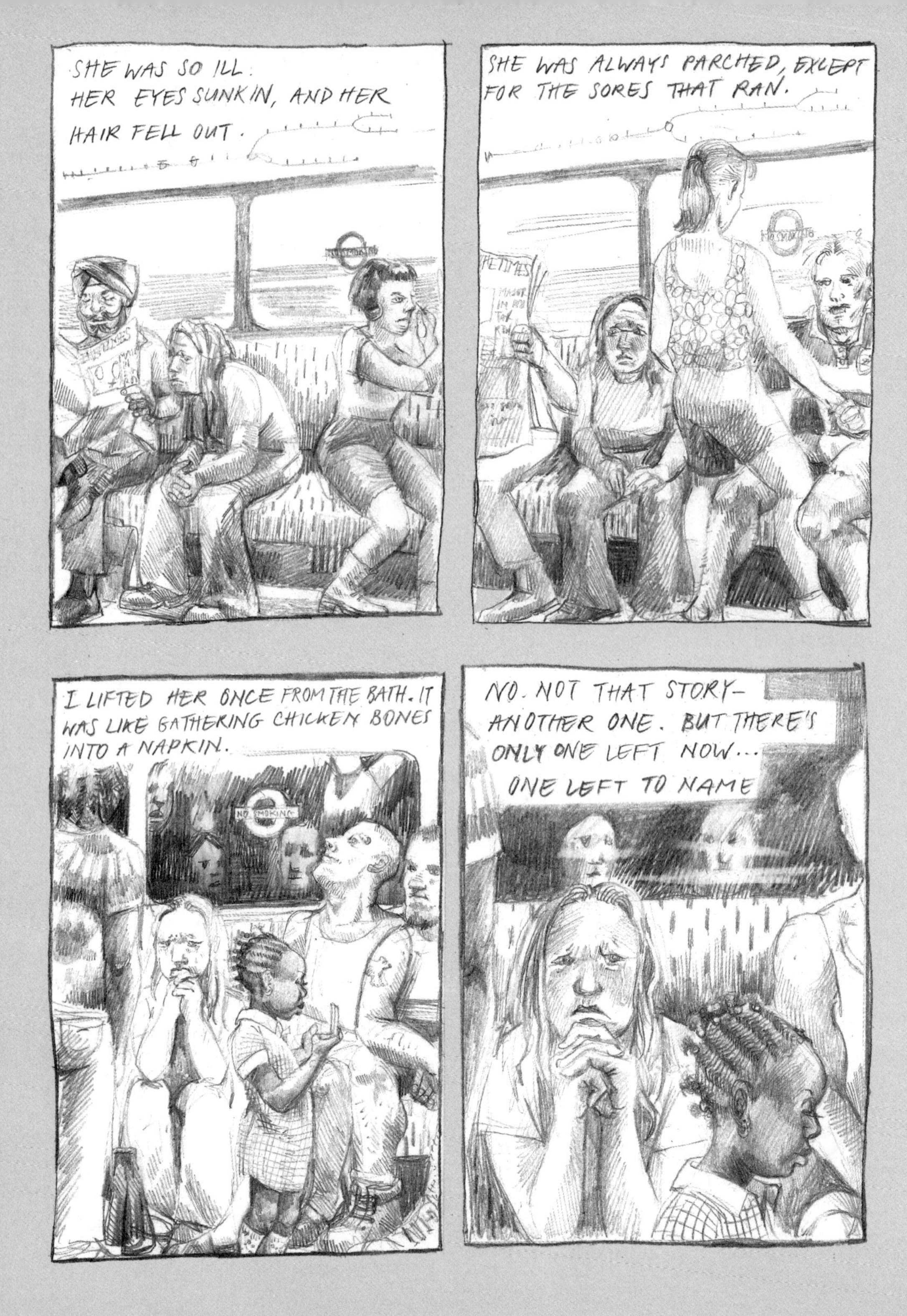
SHE WAS SO ILL.
HER EYES SUNKIN, AND HER
HAIR FELL OUT.
SHE WAS ALWAYS PARCHED, EXCEPT
FOR THE SORES THAT RAN.
I LIFTED HER ONCE FROM THE BATH. IT
WAS LIKE GATHERING CHICKEN BONES
INTO A NAPKIN.
NO SMOKING
NO. NOT THAT STORY–
ANOTHER ONE. BUT THERE'S
ONLY ONE LEFT NOW...
ONE LEFT TO NAME

NUCKELAVEE
THE SCOTS HAD A NAME FOR IT . . .

...THE UNSPEAKABLE THING. THE NUCKELAVEE.
THE DEVIL OF THE SEA.
HIS BREATH CAUSED EPIDEMICS, HIS FOOTSTEPS BLIGHT. HE WAS THE WORST OF ALL MONSTERS, AND TO MEET WITH HIM WAS DEATH.
THE DEVIL OF THE SEA ABHORRED FRESH WATER.
THE WINTER RAINS KEPT HIM IN HIDING...
...AND IN THE SUMMER, DURING THE VERDANT YEARLY REIGN OF THE MITHER O' THE SEA, HIS EVIL POWERS WERE SHACKLED...
...BUT HE WOULD ROAM WHEN THE NIGHTS WERE DRY, IN THE SEASONS IN BETWEEN.
ONE SUCH NIGHT, A MAN CALLED TAM WAS OUT WALKING...

..WHEN HE MET THE NUCKELAVEE ON THE ROAD.
BUT TAM HAD GREAT PRESENCE OF MIND.
FILLING HIS CAP FROM A BURN, HE THREW FRESH WATER AT THE MONSTER
AND AS IT SHRIEKED IN AGONY, HE JUMPED ACROSS THE STREAM TO SAFETY.
TAM HAD CHEATED DEATH AND WON.
BUT NUCKELAVEE WALKED ON.

I KNOW THIS PERSONALLY.
DEL TRIMS LTD
TAIL & WHOLESALE
431
NITA FABR
OLESALE

FRUITERER
SIMON'S
BUBBLES
LAUNDRETTE
0171 3922581
PROP: MRS E KNIGHTS
POLL
TAX

Nana
Come on, darling. Come on inside.
owaaaaaah-oooh
I want her
I want my mum
I know.
I want her too,
my girl
my little girl.

You sit tight and I'll get us some tea. It's too warm for cocoa, ain't it?
yeah, a bit

Fran! Come here and let me show you something
MUM? YOU NEED TO BE DEAD! YOU'RE NOT WELL ENOUGH. PLEASE –
Look! They let us have pets in here!
WHO LETS YOU HAVE PETS?
The Olympic Committee, of course, darling
WHAT? ARE YOU IN THE PARALYMPICS?
No, the Cancerlympics. Through here –
meet the team!
Hi, Fran
HI.

YOU'RE IN THE TEAM TOO, FRAN.
DID YOU KNOW THAT SWIMMING RUNS IN THE GENES?
WILL PATRONS' KINDLY REFRAIN FROM
RUNNING
PUSHING
SHOUTING
DUCKING
PETTING
BOMBING
SWIMMING IN DIVING AREA
SMOKING
THANK YOU!

I'M DOING THE 800M BREAST-STROKE.

Tea! You've fallen asleep.
You were having a dream, by the looks of it

Don't remember.

Alex rang. I said you'd phone her back.

'bout forty-five minutes?
yeah.
In the churchyard, then we can go in
yeah
bye

LAYING GHOSTS

THERE WAS A COTTAGE
WHICH WAS HAUNTED NIGHTLY.
THE TENANTS COULDN'T
GET A WINK OF SLEEP.

A WOMAN WAS SENT FOR; A GHOST-LAYER WHO WAS KNOWN IN THE VILLAGES. SHE WENT TO THE COTTAGE AND SET HERSELF UP BY THE HEARTH.
SHE WAS BESET BY TERRIBLE VISITATIONS...
...WHICH SHE SENT AWAY,
KNOWING THEY WERE ONLY A SCREEN FOR THE TRUE SOURCE OF THE HAUNTING

SOME HOURS BEFORE DAWN, A PALE YOUNG MAN WALKED IN.
HE STARTED TO TALK, AND THE WOMAN BORE WITNESS.
HE HAD BEEN KILLED FOR GOLD, BY THE COUPLE WHO HAD BUILT THE HOUSE, AND BEEN BURIED IN THE GARDEN. HE POINTED TO A SPOT, AND THE GHOST-LAYER SET HER THIMBLE THERE.
NEXT DAY THEY DUG UP BONES FROM BENEATH THAT SPOT IN THE GARDEN. THE BONES WERE LAID IN HOLY GROUND... AND THE COTTAGE WAS LEFT IN PEACE.

I'm going to meet Alex in a bit, do you want anything from the co-op?
Some Fairy Liquid, please, dear. And one of them beef and onion pies in a tin that I like. We'll have it for tea, shall we?
OVER MY DEAD BODY WE WILL. YUCK.
SALOON
SHE'LL BE HALF AN HOUR STILL. MIGHT AS WELL WAIT IN HERE.
DIOCESE OF SOUTHWARK
CHURCH OF
ST. MICHAEL
-THE-EAST

Excuse me – sorry. But I really want to know. What are you doing?
Ah! I am dowsing, my dear, for the lost rivers of London. The Walbrook, the Effra ...

Oh, right. I saw you in the Black Boy last night as well
Did you? Yes, I often enjoy a ginger wine or two. Been going since the 'sixties.
Has it always been called that?
Seems a bit odd, doesn't it? It's named after a ghost story. It was the Red Lion, until a little servant boy kept popping up in the cellars, crying for his mum. Poor thing. This part of London's full of ghosts...
I don't know if I believe in ghosts or not.
...Foundlings, orphans. Over there in Whitechapel, the Ripper's dark traces—
Are there just ghosts here? Any monsters, like—
Oh no, dear, there are no monsters. They are simply embodiments of human fear. The Japs after Nagasaki— Godzilla, yes? Destroyer of cities. There you go.
Oh.

My own ancestors, scrabbling for oats in the aftermath of the Highland clearances; they had one—

Nuckelavee!

Why yes! A scholarly one, by Jove.

I sort of like it here, by the church. My nan was born just down the road.

A true Cockney! I myself am a son of the Fens, lured to the metropolis as a callow youth by the bona vida.

What did you do?

I acted. I wrote. I tended the coffers of the Council in a dreary office block.

rummage
?
Would you like a sandwich? Cod roe and celery, with just a soupçon of cayenne pepper?
Ha! Oh, sorry. No thank you, you have them. I've just eaten.
Actually, I've got to go and meet my friend. Lovely meeting you.

And you.
This friend - would that be the Byronic youth of last evening?
NO - what? Did you see us in the pub, then? I thought -
One notices things on the periphery. I wouldn't pine away over that one, though. Just a hunch.

Two pints of cider and two Pernod and blacks, please
Are you sure the others both want Pernod and black? *
Yeah, I am
GIN
WHISKY
LONDON PRIDE
* A TRANSPARENT ATTEMPT TO DISGUISE THE FACT THAT WE ARE ON OUR OWN AND DRINKING 'RED WITCHES'. I DON'T KNOW IF THEY ARE ILLEGAL, BUT THEY WON'T SERVE YOU ONE
sslip
sslip
Here's to the Witch!

You see that weird tree thing over there?
Mmm?
Well... I was in there with Sam last night getting caned, and I gave him a blow job -
Oh! Mazel tov!
I knew you'd say that, you freak! You're like a proud parent about my sexual milestones.
"Tell Momma, baby - did you swallow?"
eeurgh!

Anyway, afterwards guess what he said?
Aaargh! What?
He put on a voice like Dave Lee Travis and said "Did you take it all down?"
HA HA HA HA!
"Did ya take it all down"! Ha! What a prick.
He's allright.

You know today— I mean, I know how awful it was when your mum, erm, passed away— well, I can sort of imagine if it was my mum— but... why is it so scary? Not just sad?

I don't know. I can only explain it like a monster.

Like, there's this sort of legend up north about a shape-shifting demon.

I know, one of those things that can look like a werewolf, or a spider, or a little kid. Like "It", the Stephen King book...

Exactly. Well,—it's sometimes sadness, but then it changes to the worst fear ever, or being, like, really fucking furious. It's weird.
You can't keep track of it. What a bastard.
They said at Mum's funeral, "In the midst of life we are in death."
I don't know what that means.
Nor do I really. Probably we're too young.
Maybe it's a bit like "welcome to the Jungle"...
Ha ha! Oh - that reminds me.

When you went home I saw Crap Slash again. He asked us to his gig.
He so wants to do it with you!
You're so wrong. He was actually very careful to ask you too - I reckon he thinks we're going out
Yeah, he wants to put us in a cage on stage and do a lezzer show
Yeah, right. Shall we do it?
ha ha ha ha
ooh, my eyes have gone funny from the sun
Who's that?
Him? He lives round here. He's like this brilliant zen wizard or something

What're you doing later?

Bugger all. I've got to go to the Co-op for Nana before –

Wait a minute – next-door neighbour – Hi Mrs. Philpott!

Hello, dear, how's Rene?

Fine.

Tell her I'll pop in on her later; she wanted to look at my book.

Will do.

Come on then. Lili. Good girl.
I thought you were shit-scared of dogs – that one on the golf course –
Sometimes, Alexandra, a dog is just a dog.
What's that supposed to be, an ancient Chinese proverb?
Yeah.
MISSIS
CHICKEN
HALAL
Will you be all right?
Probably not. But I'll see you tomorrow.
TO TRAINS
MP "FOUND WITH BANANA" STORM
Evening Standard

YS
AND
HOP
NO POLL TAX
HALAL
NO POLL TAX
CO OP
20P

ENTOS
ED BEEF & ONION PIE
ONLY 99p
UK

KEYS
CUT
SHOE
REPAIR

"I WASN'T A GIRL, AND I WASN'T QUITE A WOMAN.
BUT THAT SUMMER, MY ANOKAK HAD GOT
QUITE A BIT TIGHTER AROUND THE ARMS."

DIARY
1993

When I was eight or nine I discovered in my primary school library an Usborne picture book about ghosts (and if anyone has a copy please let me know). It was my poison book, like Dorian Gray's. It featured, notably, the story of Gef, the ghostly talking mongoose 'with little yellow hands' who tormented an insular farming family near Douglas in the 1930s; and a big double page about black dogs, about the phantom hounds and shape-shifting shocks, brags and barguests of rural England.

These uncanny creatures were much better and scarier to me than human-shaped ghosts with rattling chains and ruffs and things, and they were the start of an obsession with folklore, with the psychic and social function of tall tales and bogeys, which has lasted for more than 25 years.

In *Naming Monsters* Fran haphazardly catalogues a series of monsters and ghostly things which mean something to her, which help her represent the unrepresentable. They are all examples of the folkloric migratory legend: a tale which is found in diffuse locations and at different times, but which has the same plot or purpose and a similar message or function for the community of origin, despite often containing a wealth of topographical detail. An example of this is the Boggart story, given by Christina Hole in *English Folklore* as the story of 'Boggart Hole Clough', but which is told 'with much circumstantial detail of names and houses in several parts of Lancashire and Yorkshire' (Hole: 1950 pp 151–152).

Fran's monster stories represent the unrepresentable or unspeakable elements of her own experience. They are dwellers in unlit caverns, greedy for their escape into consciousness. From this vaguely psychoanalytic perspective, I found the cathartic final tale of the ghost-layer, which I have abridged from one in Katharine Briggs's *Folk Tales and Legends of the British Isles*, very interesting.

The house is haunted by a poltergeist, which then appears as a frightening demonic pig – in fact the poltergeist itself is a fake, a misleading apparition to divert from the reality of the murdered young man. These ghosts are like glamours from a fairy-ballad: Tam Lin as 'a newt or a snake' in Janet's arms; the woman transfigured into a 'grisly ghost...with teeth like tether-stakes' to whom stout-hearted King Henry pays court. They also work like screen memories or dream-images. They have a quality which reminds me of the Wolfman's (Freud's patient Sergei Pankejeff) haunting dream of white wolves in a tree – something which because it is uncanny in itself is enough to disturb, to hold the interest like a decoy, an armless man of the subconscious – and which would allow the repression of the truth were it not for the ghost-layer (or analyst) herself.

As usual, for Fran, the truth is what she knew all along.

I recently saw an American TV programme called *Paranormal Witness*. Presented in a documentary style with *Crimewatch*-style 'reconstructions', it told the 'true story' of a driver who stopped on a New England country road for what appeared to be a sobbing high school girl who was crouched on the greensward, but, when the figure turned around, she was seen to have no face.

This is a brilliant example of the contemporary transmission of the migratory legend. Lafcadio Hearn documented old Japanese stories of the Mujina, a faceless ghost, in the 1904 *Kwaidan* (Weird Tales): she also featured, with convincing topographical detail, in a Hawaiian newspaper after several sightings in the bathroom at a drive-in cinema in 1950s Honolulu.

Paranormal Witness uses the layered manipulation of TV signifiers: for instance, the acting styles and costumes used to denote the separation of 'traumatised real-life witness' and 'actor playing witness in the reconstruction'. These serve as a replacement for the traditional devices around the oral transmission of a tale to get the listeners to suspend their disbelief – a hearth on a winter's night, for instance, or the statement that 'this happened to a friend of a friend'.

Although *Naming Monsters* explores the subjective psychic function of monsters for one individual rather than as an expression of the fears of a society, the point of the migratory legend is that it does precisely this, and functions as an archetype.

I once worked on some therapeutic story-writing with an eight-year-old boy who came from a very unsafe home and had been coached not to talk. He produced a story called *The Gremlin* (he had never heard any folk stories and I hazard a guess that this name came from the 1985 film *Gremlins* or its sequels). *The Gremlin* was about a house haunted in its very fabric, in the walls and in the gaps between the floorboards, by an invisible creature that persecuted the family and hid in their luggage when they tried to leave. It was so unbelievably similar to 'Boggart Hole Clough' that I decided to read him a version afterwards, telling him about myths. He was breathless with his own power, repeating disbelievingly, 'I'm a storyteller!' (He was.)

Of course, the Internet is the ideal conduit for the transmission of vernacular half-belief, of fireside tales and what used to be oral lore (see Shuckland.com for an excellent catalogue of black dog sightings). It has, as far as I can see, generated a brand new migratory legend archetype with the Black-Eyed Kids phenomenon. This resembles a European vampire legend or Haitian zombie myth but is really a modern embodiment of the fear of killer adolescence: uncannily self-possessed teenage children try to infiltrate urban domestic spaces, leading to the 'certain death' of the occupant. It was started with a posting on Obiwan's Paranormal Page in 1998 by Brian Bethel, and is now an Internet folklore phenomenon, with many 'survivors' claiming to have been accosted by these confident kids with no sclera or pupil, just 'deep black pools', who give off a prickling sense of evil.

In the Kentish secondary school where I worked eight years ago, a paranormal website called S.F.O.G.S. was a big fad amongst the younger boys; once, one of them urgently called me over – 'Look, miss, they've found a real mermaid!' Marvelling at the persistence of these things, I saw a photo of a shoddy yet alarming chimerical creature – half a dried monkey grafted onto a fishtail – that was identical to Phineus T. Barnum's famous FeeJee Mermaid hoax of 1842. Gaping at it round the school computer, the boys could have been their counterparts of a century and a half before, standing at the showman's barrow.

These kinds of stories seem able to co-exist alongside, and separately from, urban legends. The story of the Black-Eyed Kids, for example, is somehow unlike that of the murdered co-ed whose killer writes, in her blood, to her roommate, 'Aren't you glad you didn't turn the light on?'

Most urban legends have a bloody resolution and often an element of normative or repressive morality. There are many warnings for women who risk lone outings in suburban hinterlands, go too far with their boyfriends or engage in sexual thrill-seeking. They play on the urban fear of the other, of the breaking of body and space boundaries through literal, abject means, and there is something stark and pornographic about them. Stories of ghosts and monsters, although they serve to frighten, help us preserve a sense of wonder. We can own them; they can take up residence inside us and create poetic and important resonances that help us deal – especially as children – with those things that remain so hard to say.

Hannah Eaton, March 2013

ACKNOWLEDGEMENTS

Huge thanks to Corinne Pearlman for having faith in the (frankly weird) first draft and making this experience a real adventure. Your sensitivity and expertise have been invaluable.

To Candida Lacey for all her support; Vicky, Holly, Linda and Adrian at Myriad.

To Daniel Locke and Hannah Chater, Paul O'Connell, Lawrence Elwick, Tanya Meditzsky and Joe Flavell for comics advice, inspiration and friendship.

Hannah Berry; Jessica Salazar and her truly superior skill-set; Andrew, for the Ministry of Friendship.

Alex, Catherine, Catherine, Chloe (for the golf course), Corin, Fran (for your generosity), Gaby, Helena, Kev, Lindi, Mathew, Richard (for the upside-down horse and the perfect duvet), Simon, Sue, (not to mention Lorraine, Chris, Yogashwara and Griphook) and Vicki.

Lucia, Rafael, Gabriel and Luca for a new generation of scary stories.

Tom, Vicky, Ellie, Isobel and Jessica for being them. And Tom, thank you for letting me make fiction out of things that are partly yours.

A note on the text: 'Beware of the Kappa' signs, like the one on page 30, are still common in rural and suburban Japan.

MORE GRAPHICS FROM MYRIAD EDITIONS